Samuel French Acting Editic

MW00655208

What We're Up Against

by Theresa Rebeck

‖SAMUEL FRENCH‖

ISBN 978-0-573-70167-2

www.concordtheatricals.com
www.concordtheatricals.co.uk

FOR PRODUCTION INQUIRIES

UNITED STATES AND CANADA
info@concordtheatricals.com
1-866-979-0447

UNITED KINGDOM AND EUROPE
licensing@concordtheatricals.co.uk
020-7054-7200

Each title is subject to availability from Concord Theatricals Corp., depending upon country of performance. Please be aware that *WHAT WE'RE UP AGAINST* may not be licensed by Concord Theatricals Corp. in your territory. Professional and amateur producers should contact the nearest Concord Theatricals Corp. office or licensing partner to verify availability.

This work is published by Samuel French, an imprint of Concord Theatricals Corp.

No one shall make any changes in this title(s) for the purpose of production. No part of this book may be reproduced, stored in a retrieval system, scanned, uploaded, or transmitted in any form, by any means, now known or yet to be invented, including mechanical, electronic, digital, photocopying, recording, videotaping, or otherwise, without the prior written permission of the publisher. No one shall share this title(s), or any part of this title(s), through any social media or file hosting websites.

For all inquiries regarding motion picture, television, online/digital and other media rights, please contact Concord Theatricals Corp.

MUSIC AND THIRD-PARTY MATERIALS USE NOTE

Licensees are solely responsible for obtaining formal written permission from copyright owners to use copyrighted music and/or other copyrighted third-party materials (e.g., artworks, logos) in the performance of this play and are strongly cautioned to do so. If no such permission is obtained by the licensee, then the licensee must use only original music and materials that the licensee owns and controls. Licensees are solely responsible and liable for clearances of all third-party copyrighted materials, including without limitation music, and shall indemnify the copyright owners of the play(s) and their licensing agent, Concord Theatricals Corp., against any costs, expenses, losses and liabilities arising from the use of such copyrighted third-party materials by licensees. For music, please contact the appropriate music licensing authority in your territory for the rights to any incidental music.

IMPORTANT BILLING AND CREDIT REQUIREMENTS

If you have obtained performance rights to this title, please refer to your licensing agreement for important billing and credit requirements.

WHAT WE'RE UP AGAINST was first produced by Magic Theatre (Loretta Greco, Artistic Director) in San Francisco on February 9, 2011. The performance was directed by Loretta Greco, with sets by Skip Mercier, costumes by Alex Jaeger, lights by Sarah Sidman, and sound by Sara Huddleston. The cast was as follows:

STU..Warren David Keith

BEN ....Rod Gnapp

ELIZA.. Sarah Nealis

JANICE .... Pamela Gaye Walker

WEBER ....James Wagner

WHAT WE'RE UP AGAINST premiered Off Broadway at the WP Theater in New York City by special arrangement with Segal NYC Productions on October 28, 2017. The performance was directed by Adrienne Campbell-Holt, with sets by Narelle Sissons, costumes by Tilly Grimes, lights by Grant Yeager, and sound by M.L. Dogg. The production stage manager was Katie Young. The cast was as follows:

STU... Damian Young

BEN ....Jim Parrack

ELIZA..Krysta Rodriguez

JANICE .... Marg Helgenberger

WEBER ....Skylar Astin

CHARACTERS

STU

BEN

ELIZA

JANICE

WEBER

ACT ONE

Scene One

(Stu's office. **STU** *and* **BEN** *sit at a drafting table.* **STU** *reaches into the bottom drawer of a file cabinet, finds a bottle of scotch, and pours drinks.)*

STU. All I'm saying is there's –

BEN. Rules. That's what I'm trying to –

STU. A system.

BEN. Yes, Jesus, I –

STU. Things don't just happen, history, events –

BEN. I know, this is not –

STU. We create.

BEN. Exactly. A company. I tried to –

STU. You look at anything, the Boy Scouts, some fucking convent, and maybe it doesn't seem like –

BEN. You just can't –

STU. It's part of something much more complicated. You can't just act like that's not true.

BEN. That's my point. Women are always just a total fucking nightmare. That's all I'm saying.

STU. I'm not saying that. That is not what –

BEN. Okay, okay, fine, but –

STU. You cannot give them that.

BEN. I'm not giving them anything. I'm just saying –

STU. Look, they want to work, women want to work, they should have the opportunity. Jesus, that's what, you got to be careful saying shit like that. Because it's all over the news, they're talking to reporters and whining it's

7

so unfair, we're threatened, we don't like them, when
that's not what's going on. You can't give them that.

BEN. Stu, you just said she –

STU. She tricked me. That is my point. She is a lying,
deceitful, dishonest little manipulator. I don't mind
working with her. But, she is a bitch. That, I mind.

BEN. That's what I'm –

STU. No, that is not what you're saying, Ben. These are two
very different things. I welcomed her. I mean it's the
nineties! It's time, you know? Let's get some new blood
in here! So I was happy when they hired her, I said, I
want to work with this woman.

BEN. Oh, come on –

STU. Excuse me?

BEN. What? I'm just saying –

STU. What are you saying, Ben?

BEN. I'm saying, shit, I'm saying you didn't want her any
more than the rest of us. What do we need another
woman for? Janice is one, we have one, / I don't know
what we need to stockpile women for.

STU. This isn't an issue of sex. That's what I'm telling you.
Are you listening to me?

BEN. Yes, I'm listening, you're not –

STU. It's the system I'm talking about. It's not whether or
not she's a woman. It's the fact that she has no respect,
this is my point. She comes into my office and says, "We
need to talk, Stu," and I'm, okay, I'm fine, I can talk,
I don't have a problem with this. She has questions.
I'm fine with this. She wants to know why I won't
let her work. Now, that is not what is happening, I
explain that to her. She is a new employee, how long
has she been here, five months, six months, this is not
– the experience isn't there. That is my point. When
the experience is there, she'll be put on projects. She
wants to know how she can get the experience if she's
not on a project. This is a good question. And so I tell
her: Initiative. Initiative, that is how the system works,

that is how America works, this is what they don't understand. No one hands you things. You work for them. You earn them. You prove yourself worthy. So she says to me, "What about Weber?" And I say, "What about him?" And she says, "You let him work. He's been here four months, and you put him on projects."

BEN. Oh, that is –

STU. Exactly. She's jealous. She doesn't care about the work, she just cares, she's competitive, Weber got ahead of her and she doesn't like it. So I say to her, "That's got nothing to do with you. This isn't about competition. This is about business. We use the best person for the job. If you prove yourself, through initiative, to be the best person, to be worthy, we will use you."

BEN. So what'd she say to –

STU. I'll tell you what she said. This, she tells me, she stopped by Weber's office and picked up a copy of that mall extension you guys are working on, the Roxbury project –

BEN. What? What'd she do that for?

STU. So she's got your design, right –

BEN. That thing's not finished, Stu. Did she show you that? She had no business doing that. We are not finished with that.

STU. So she says to me –

BEN. I cannot believe her, trying to make us look bad! We haven't solved the duct thing yet, okay, we're still working on it! I can't believe –

STU. Would you shut up, Ben? I'm trying to explain something to you. She's not after your balls, she's after Weber –

BEN. I'm just saying, we're still working on that. We've got ideas.

STU. I'm not talking about your ideas, Ben, I'm trying to tell you something! She brings me your design, she tells me she got it from Weber, and then she says, "I can see putting Ben on this, he's got seniority. But why does Weber get to work, and not me? What is so good about what he does?" She's pissing me off now, because I explained this to her, it's not about competition, I said that, but if she wants to play this game, fine, I'll show her why Weber got the project. So I go through it. Every detail. I show her how every detail indicates that Weber has experience. I prove it to her. And you know what she says to me? "I designed that."

BEN. What?

STU. She put Weber's name on one of her designs. She came up with her own fucking design for that fucking mall, and then she pretended it was Weber's. She tricked me.

BEN. You're shitting me.

STU. This fucking woman stands there – she stands there, and says to me, "This is my point, Stu. It's not about the work, it's about point of view. When a woman designs it, it's shit, and when a man designs it, it's great." So I say to her, "No this isn't about point of view, this is about power. You're trying to cut off my balls here." She says, "Look at the design, Stu, you know it's good," and I say, "I don't give a shit if it's good. You want to play by these rules, I can play by these rules. It's shit. Get out of my face."

BEN. You said that? Unbelievable.

STU. This is what we're up against.

BEN. Fuck.

(Pause. They think about this.)

But it was good?

STU. What?

BEN. The design. You said –

STU. Fuck you, are you fucking listening to a word I'm saying?

BEN. Yes, I'm listening, I just – I was wondering what she did with the air ducts.

STU. What? What are you saying?

BEN. I'm saying, you know, Weber and I – those fucking ducts are all over the entryway there, and we can't –

STU. Fuck you, Ben, you are not listening to a word out of my mouth.

BEN. Yeah, I know, she's a bitch, she's a fucking nightmare, but I got to tell you there were like three renovations of that mall over the last how many years, all of them by lunatics if you ask me. It's a total quandary. Weber and I have been going over that fucking duct thing for weeks and we can't crack it. So, if she's got a solution, I want to see it. Did she have a solution or not?

STU. Yeah. She did.

BEN. Well, I want to see it.

STU. No.

BEN. She's here now, fuck, they hired her and we had nothing to say about it, she's being paid, why shouldn't we use her?

STU. I'll tell you why. Because then, she's won. She didn't wait. She didn't play by the rules. It's context. If she had waited, it would've been different. If she had respect for the system. But she has no respect. This is what we're up against.

BEN. That's a load of shit, Stu.

STU. I'm what? Excuse me, did you, what did you –

BEN. Look, Stu –

STU. If she were here, listening to us, you know what she'd do?

BEN. Hopefully, she'd tell me what she did with those fucking ducts!

STU. No. That is not what she'd do. I'll tell you what she'd do. Two men, having a simple conversation, we're having drinks. Right? Is there anything wrong with this? But she sits here and she listens to us, and then she goes and tells her little friends. She goes back and she says, "They said this, and they said that, they called me a bitch, they said bad words," and she and her friends, they all go and have their groups and their meetings and complain about this, like this is some big fucking point. But there is no point, Ben. This is what they don't understand. There is a system. Things fit together. It's not about point of view. It's just about the way things are. They want things to be the way they're not. They don't get it, and they're trying to make us pay for that. But they are not going to win.

(Blackout.)

Scene Two

(**ELIZA** and **JANICE** in Janice's office. **JANICE** is working on something on a drawing board.)

ELIZA. Motherfucker.

(A beat.)

Cocksucker.

(A beat.)

Motherfucking cocksucking cocksucker.

JANICE. Okay.

ELIZA. What? He is a motherfucking cocksucking fucked up piece of shit. I fucking hate that guy. I hate him.

(**JANICE** goes to the door and looks around.)

JANICE. What happened?

ELIZA. Nothing happened. He did the same nothing that he always does. He *ignores* me. He won't let me do anything. He won't let me *do anything*. I sit there, back in that shitty little office they gave me, they gave me the worst office on the floor and I don't complain. Who cares if you have a shitty office, that's not what I, I came here to *work*. I turned down three other, everybody told me this place was just a ma*chine* there is so much to do there you'll be learning everything there is to know about everything, they don't have time to, you'll just be worked to *death* over there and you'll learn *everything* and I was like, bring it on! Everybody told me that. And he won't let me do ANYTHING. I have been here for five MONTHS and they are paying me to sit back in that shitty fucking office and do NOTHING.

JANICE. Okay. First of all, I like your office.

ELIZA. Oh for fuck's sake!

JANICE. I do I think it's cozy!

ELIZA. No it is; it's very cozy and such a convenient location, all the way down at the end of the hallway like that.

JANICE. You have a lot of privacy, *I* think that's nice.

ELIZA. Janice, Ben's assistant has a better office than me. Everybody's assistant has a better office than me! Those fucking cubicles with no fucking privacy at all are nicer than that broom closet they stuck me in. And *Weber* got a much better office and he got here AFTER me so don't tell me –

JANICE. Oh I don't like his office.

ELIZA. I'm in a broom closet! He has a wet bar!

JANICE. He has a wet bar?

ELIZA. Okay it's a lateral file but that's what he uses it for.

JANICE. So is that what you did, you told Stu that you wanted a wet bar in your office?

ELIZA. I told him I wanted to work.

JANICE. You did.

ELIZA. Yes I did.

JANICE. You said, "I want to work."

ELIZA. YES I DID I SAID "LET ME WORK."

JANICE. And what did he say?

ELIZA. He didn't say anything!

JANICE. That's good –

ELIZA. How is that good?

JANICE. That means he's thinking about it.

ELIZA. He's not thinking about it!

JANICE. Yes he is, maybe not thinking but making it look like he's thinking.

ELIZA. That's not what he's doing.

JANICE. It is it's what he does! That's his way. He likes to make it seem like his decision. It's good, that he said nothing. That's very good. When he says nothing, it's perfect.

ELIZA. Well…he didn't say nothing.

JANICE. You said he didn't say anything.

ELIZA. He said some things.

JANICE. What did he say?

ELIZA. It's complicated.

JANICE. Complicated how?

ELIZA. Complicated full of shit complicated is how.

JANICE. Okay.

ELIZA. Complicated because he is a fucking asshole complicated.

JANICE. Except.

ELIZA. I hate that fucking cocksucker.

JANICE. Is that the most useful position you can take?

ELIZA. I don't give a shit about useful; he's an asshole as well as a talent-free shithead.

JANICE. Okay. Look. I know it's frustrating. I can see that you're frustrated. But really, you should know, they love you here.

ELIZA. They what?

JANICE. They love you. I was just talking to Ben, he says they really love you.

ELIZA. Ben told you they love me?

JANICE. Just this morning. And I heard Stu say it too, they love you! They were talking to Ronald.

ELIZA. Who's Ronald?

JANICE. Weber? Ronald Weber?

ELIZA. That's his name? Ronald?

JANICE. Okay, look. If you want people to like you here –

ELIZA. What I want –

JANICE. Then maybe you could be bothered to learn their names –

ELIZA. – Is to *work* and I do know their names and nobody calls Weber "Ronald" everyone calls him Weber! He's Weber! He's not Ronald! He's Weber!

JANICE. I'm just –

ELIZA. Was there anybody else in on this lovefest?

JANICE. Yes as a matter of fact there was. David was there.

ELIZA. David was there?

JANICE. Yes, David was there and he was the one who asked.

ELIZA. Asked what.

JANICE. He asked how you were getting along. And Stu
    said –

ELIZA. Wait a minute. David was here? Where is here?

JANICE. In the kitchen.

ELIZA. David was here in the kitchen?

JANICE. Yes, and he's a fan of yours too. So I don't know
    what you're so worked up about.

ELIZA. I'm worked up because that cocksucker Stu won't let
    me do anything and he's put me in the shittiest office in
    the building and now everybody's lying about it.

JANICE. Oh really.

ELIZA. Oh really what?

JANICE. Nothing! But if people were running around
    saying they love me I don't think I'd accuse them of
    being liars. I think there's maybe a little self-esteem
    issue involved here.

ELIZA. Self-esteem?

JANICE. Just my observation.

ELIZA. Well, here's my observation. If they are running
    around saying they love me, I'd say they're lying for
    some reason and that means something's up.

> *(She goes to the door and sticks her head out,
> looking around.)*

JANICE. You are really sounding paranoid.

ELIZA. I'm sounding paranoid because I am paranoid.

> *(Then.)*

David does love me. David thinks I'm awesome. That's
why I got hired, because it's his company and he loves
me.

JANICE. Okay wait. You cannot talk to David about this.

ELIZA. About what?

JANICE. About whatever you think the problem is with Stu.

ELIZA. I thought there wasn't a problem with Stu. Stu loves
    me, I thought you just told me there wasn't a problem
    because Stu loves me.

JANICE. Yes I did say that and I am not saying there is a problem. You are the one who thinks there's a problem.

ELIZA. You know there's a problem!

JANICE. I don't know there's a problem.

ELIZA. Then why are you telling me not to talk to David about it?

JANICE. Do you want to be labeled a whiner?

ELIZA. I'm not a whiner.

JANICE. If you go to David you will be.

ELIZA. I didn't say I was going to David!

JANICE. Well, don't. Just let Stu think about this. It's good you talked to him, and it's good that David loves you, and that they are all talking about how much they love you. All of those are good things. I think it's true that it's taking a little longer than usual for them to get used to you, there's always a period of time when people don't know each other, in a firm where all of the work is project-based it makes sense that people want to work with people they know and trust and let's face it men in our field are not notorious for including women in their little *club*, but they do, eventually, it is my experience that they do eventually realize that we have something to offer and patience is as we know a virtue.

ELIZA. Is it?

JANICE. So we have been told.

ELIZA. I just never bought that.

JANICE. Why does that not surprise me.

ELIZA. Well, how long did it take you? Before they started letting you.

JANICE. It took a long time.

ELIZA. How long?

JANICE. If you have to ask you are not being patient enough.

ELIZA. I never said I was patient. I never claimed that that was one of my virtues.

JANICE. Well, that's a good thing.

(JANICE sighs. She goes back to her drawing.
ELIZA sits there and watches her.)

ELIZA. Look. I appreciate you letting me blow off steam. I really do.

JANICE. You're welcome.

ELIZA. I'll try to be more patient.

JANICE. I think that's wise.

ELIZA. Yeah. I just – sorry. I mean it's nineteen ninety-two.

JANICE. Yes. It's nineteen ninety-two.

ELIZA. You kind of thought this stuff wouldn't be going on anymore.

(A beat. JANICE doesn't even answer that one.
ELIZA sidles over.)

So what's this? They still have you doing that shitty law office in Ohio?

JANICE. That's on hold. They moved me over to this mall renovation. Ben and Ronald have been on it for weeks, and they haven't been able to do a thing with it. So Stu asked me to help them out with it.

ELIZA. You're helping them. With the mall renovation.

JANICE. He asked me this morning to take a look at it.

(A beat.)

I don't know *what* we're supposed to do with all these ducts.

(Blackout.)

Scene Three

(**WEBER**, **BEN**, *and* **JANICE** *in the conference room.* **WEBER** *holds forth.*)

WEBER. Where there is no history, we create history because history is a construct in which commerce can take place. Commerce. Malls. Malls. History! And that doesn't mean, okay, there's no question people can live without, you look at the strip malls of LA, the giant box culture of the midwest, those places survive and even thrive at times, with no gesture whatsoever to the more inchoate yearnings toward time and space. The human heart meets the void in those places and shops anyway, that's just true. But you can't, there's a cultural question which rises out of that that that aesthetic degradation which posits that nihilistic shopping is what we want, is what we are. We can tolerate it, yes; as a species we can tolerate shopping in just like a giant – whatever. But the three of us are here in this room because somebody somewhere believes we can do better. If strip malls were all we needed, really? That would be all that's out there. And it's not. I mean, even the Mall of America, which is an enormous testament to the conviction that buying and selling is what matters, not the thing bought or sold, and that what is relevant is just the pilgrimage to the place, to the temple of mammon, people coming just to worship the act of shopping – even there, there is history. Seriously, we should get a copy of their layout, it's absolutely mindblowing, what they put together out there. And how brilliant that it's in Minnesota! The heartland. It redefines from the center the meaning of America. The bonfire, the town green, the shopping mall, the place where people meet to share a meal, where teenagers come to flirt and fall in love, where children run and old people take their walks. This is more than space and time but space and time give context, you know, and everything that belongs in this space and time needs to be held there by history. Because history may be a fiction, but it's a sustainable fiction. And that's what's so brilliant about these moments, that you get to ask yourself, what kind of fiction? What kind of history? Is it...Renaissance Italy? Is it the American Southwest? 'Cause to my mind the Plaza in Kansas City is truly the greatest mall ever built. Is it Times Square? Paris after the war? It's up to us, guys. What time and space and reality do we want to create, that will hold the human spirit up, when people come here, to shop?

       (**JANICE** *and* **BEN** *look at him.*)

JANICE. That is incredible, that you put it like that is so brilliant.

WEBER. Thanks, Janice.

JANICE. I'm completely blown away.

BEN. Yeah me too. So have either of you had any thoughts about the duct situation over at the south entrance?

Because to my mind before we start addressing more abstract concerns, time, space, that sort of direction, I'd really like to be able to nail down what we're going to do with all these ducts.

WEBER. Yeah, I know you think that Ben. And I know you came up through the ranks in the general contractor's office before you condescended to study architecture like the rest of us, so you always want to jump to practicalities, but these other questions keep coming back to me and I just can't help but wondering if the problem isn't that we've skipped a step, we need to let the thinking go completely outside the box here and while we're looking over here, the answer will come from over there. Because you know I have been thinking about why, why, why why is it such a puzzle? It's turned into its own, it's like a Chinese box of torment, maybe we should see the place as a Chinese palace, the Forbidden City, what would those ducts look like if the context was thirteenth century imperial China?

BEN. Like dog shit.

(A beat.)

JANICE. Okay wait. So you want to redesign the whole mall as the Forbidden City, like, from China?

WEBER. Reimagine, why not?

JANICE. Well, it's just a lot of Americans are a little intimidated by China right now and there's all that stuff on the news about how China is going to own America pretty soon and I don't know, don't we think that will scare people?

WEBER. Scare people away from shopping? I don't think that's possible.

BEN. The larger question being, what do we do with those ducts. Because my sense is, Stu is really concerned about that.

WEBER. He's fine.

BEN. He's not really all that fine. I talked to him last night, and he was concerned.

JANICE. What about Venice? Not Venice California but Venice Italy. Stone steps everywhere and tiny little cul-de-sacs with shops and then suddenly you make a wrong turn and you find yourself in a food court that looks just like a piazza, with a fountain and Neptune in the middle of it, with his scepter.

WEBER. Janice is having a moment with Neptune and his scepter, I don't know Janice, I think I'm feeling a little sexually harassed here –

JANICE. Stop it, I think this could work –

BEN. Something like a mini-Disneyland version of Venice.

JANICE. Yes. Don't they have places like that in Vegas?

WEBER. Now we're going to Vegas! I'm definitely being harassed.

JANICE. Do you think people would like to go to a place like that?

BEN. Do people go to Vegas? Yes my sense is that a lot of people do in fact make the occasional pilgrimage to Vegas for things like casinos and gambling and getting completely shitfaced and picking up prostitutes.

WEBER. And shopping.

BEN. Yeah, I'm sure they shop there as well. So what, uh, what –

WEBER. I think this is a good area. Good job, Janice.

JANICE. Thanks.

WEBER. Areas, areas, China, Vegas, areas wait a minute I have another idea. What if we considered the whole Vegas experiment as a model for the project.

BEN. *(A shred of impatience.)* A "model" for what project?

WEBER. For the mall, the Roxbury mall, isn't that what we're talking about?

BEN. Yes, I was just making sure because you know they're not looking for a complete rethinking. They want to expand six thousand square feet into the southeast parking area and enclose the area that abuts the northwest intersection. If you go back to the specs –

WEBER. I'm not talking about the specs.

BEN. I know you're not. That's why I brought it up. I think it's important to consider the specs here.

WEBER. But this is my point. I don't want to talk about the specs.

BEN. This is *my* point. I do want to talk about the specs. I want to talk about how to dismantle the sprinkler system without shutting down the air conditioning. I want to know what fucking moron put the steam line into the wall instead of the ceiling, it's not like there wasn't room up there. And the plumbing lines have to stay in place so how do we manage to move everything else?

WEBER. Why are you so frustrated?

BEN. I'm – frustrated – because we've been going around about this for a long time, Weber, a really long time and last night Stu got a little pissed off –

WEBER. Pissed off? You said he was concerned.

BEN. Yeah, he's concerned and pissed off.

WEBER. He didn't tell me about it.

BEN. He's not pissed off at you.

WEBER. But he's pissed off about this project?

BEN. Yes he is. In fact he is.

WEBER. Why?

BEN. Because he wants that duct thing solved! He wants it solved now.

JANICE. Is he pissed off with me? Because I wasn't even on this, I just got the call this morning, that he wanted me to come over and give you a hand on this.

BEN. He's not pissed at you.

WEBER. So he's pissed at you.

BEN. Look, could we just get back to, what we have to do, what we really have to do here, is figure out what we are going to do about all those fucking ducts! Does anyone have an idea about those ducts! I would really like a little brainstorming around the ducts.

(Silence. No one says anything.)

Oh that's great.

WEBER. Listen. Listen! We clearly are not ready to discuss the ducts. I don't know why there is this irrational fixation on this one narrow aspect of an enormously nuanced and complicated series of questions about this mall. Yes, we have a problem with the ducts. We also have questions about aesthetics, about history, culture, commerce –

BEN. Okay, except there is a time constraint here.

WEBER. People say there are time constraints all the time, which is fine, if the answer shows up, but if the answer *doesn't* show up in that time frame? It just isn't there.

JANICE. Can't argue with that.

BEN. Yeah, but the right answer did show up! It did show up and now we're fucked! So we have to figure this out NOW. If we don't figure this out now we are in major trouble! Stu is PISSED OFF. And if we don't figure out how to solve the problem of what to do with those fucking ducts NOW, people are going to be FIRED.

WEBER. Okay. Okay. You clearly have some information that you have not been sharing with the team here. Such as...there is a solution on the table?

   (A beat.)

   You just said, I think that it had been solved, didn't you say that?

BEN. Yeah, I said it.

WEBER. So what are we arguing about?

BEN. It's hard to explain.

WEBER. But there is a solution.

BEN. Yeah, there is.

WEBER. So when'd you come up with it?

BEN. I didn't come up with it.

WEBER. Janice? Did you come up with it?

JANICE. Honestly I'm having a little trouble following this. I just started looking at this today! I thought this was a kind of hello get to know each other on this project kind of situation. So I don't, I mean, I didn't come up with any solutions today because I thought today was just like, hello.

WEBER. Okay. I didn't come up with it, and you didn't come up with it and Janice clearly didn't come up with it. So who came up with it?

BEN. *(A beat.)* Eliza Newsom went into your office and found the specs. Then she went to her office and came up with her own design about how one might construct an extension into the southeast parking lot and enclose the walkways up by the northwest intersection, and included in her design there is in fact a solution to the question, what do you do with those fucking air ducts which are all over the southeastern entryway, which we need to fold into the design of the extension, in a manner that is both practical and aesthetic.

WEBER. *She* solved it.

BEN. Yes she did.

WEBER. Eliza? Solved it.

BEN. Yes.

WEBER. Fuck her, it's not even her project!

BEN. No, it's not.

WEBER. I knew she was pissed when they put me on this.

BEN. She was.

WEBER. I heard her in the kitchen – she was talking to you, actually, Janice, and she said some things that were pretty, I mean, I didn't confront her, or you, I understand she's jealous. That's not my problem. But this, just walking into Stu's office and trying to take over my project, that is unacceptable. Completely off the table. Fucking bitch. No offense Janice.

JANICE. No, I know, it's upsetting. I had no idea.

WEBER. Did she talk to you about this?

JANICE. No, no –

WEBER. Come on –

JANICE. She would not talk to me about something like that because she knows I would absolutely not support her in that!

WEBER. You guys talk to each other.

JANICE. Yes we talk to each other but not about, we talk to each other about things like lunch, and – makeup and shoes. She didn't tell me anything about any of this. Because if she did I would have told her – come on, this is so unprofessional. I don't –

WEBER. *(To* **BEN***.)* So she went in and tried to get me kicked off this. That is totally unacceptable.

BEN. That's not what she did.

WEBER. Then what did she do?

BEN. She was pissed off, apparently –

WEBER. She's always pissed off. Everything pisses her off.

BEN. Because she didn't have anything to do.

WEBER. Who wants to work with her? She's a fucking nightmare!

BEN. So she did this design and told Stu it was yours –

WEBER. She WHAT?

> *(Turning on* **JANICE**.*)*

And you didn't know about this?

JANICE. Of course not! I'm not kidding you guys. If she had told me, I would have told her not to. God. She pretended –

BEN. She pretended. And she got Stu to tell her that her design was good. Because he thought it was Weber's.

WEBER. He told her it was good?

BEN. That's what he said. Apparently, it was pretty good.

WEBER. So he saw it.

BEN. Yeah he looked at it. And he thought it was yours, and he said it was good, and then she told him it wasn't yours.

WEBER. Fucking bitch. No offense Janice.

JANICE. *(Agreeing with him.)* Please! I can't believe she wasn't fired for that.

WEBER. Has she been fired?

BEN. Not to my knowledge, no.

WEBER. Why didn't he fire her?

BEN. I don't know. I don't think this would rise to cause –

WEBER. She lied! How much more cause do you need than that? She lied!

BEN. I don't know.

WEBER. Fucking bitch. No offense Janice.

JANICE. It's okay.

WEBER. This is all David you know. She's sleeping with David. That's how she even got this job.

BEN. It doesn't matter how she got this job.

WEBER. That's how she got it, right, Janice?

JANICE. I have no idea.

WEBER. It's totally how she got the job.

BEN. *(Abrupt, frustrated.)* It doesn't matter how she got the job because she is here now and the thing is, frankly, frankly, the problem we have now is that she did in fact solve the duct thing. And Stu saw it! He saw it and he went through it and he LOOKED at it and now he can't remember it. Or, if he does remember it which honestly I don't think he does, he's too mad about it to to to – no. No! He doesn't remember it! He was probably drunk when he looked at it. Don't tell him I said that. Fuck. The bottom line is, Stu knows there's a solution out there, and we need that solution. But he doesn't want to ask her for it. And he doesn't want us to ask her for it.

WEBER. Of course not! Christ, that would be like admitting she was right! Fuck her!

BEN. That's the position.

WEBER. So where's the design now?

BEN. I didn't ask. Presumably, she has it.

WEBER. Well, fuck her! We can solve this! If she can, we certainly can.

BEN. I've always thought that. There's a solution out there, there's more than one even. There's always a solution. We just have to figure out what it is. On a clock. Stu's kind of in not a great mood about this. That's why, he would really like us to put our attention on it because he's feeling kind of like he got played and it makes him feel stupid and he'd like to put it behind him, and if we could just untangle this little issue around the ducts as quickly as possible, really really quickly, that would make him feel better I think, just quickly.

WEBER. Of course.

BEN. Yeah.

> (*There is a moment of silence.* **WEBER** *looks at the blueprints.*)

WEBER. Maybe we could...

> (*He turns them around, thinks. Gives up.* **JANICE** *goes up to look at them. She smiles at* **WEBER**.)

JANICE. I'm sure we can solve this.

WEBER. Absolutely.

> *(She stares at it.)*

JANICE. Maybe... What happens if we just take them all out? Just yank them out? As a start.

BEN. The heating and the cooling systems for the entire complex break down as well as all the refrigeration units in the food service areas.

> *(**BEN** looks up in the air while she considers this.)*

JANICE. Hmmmm.

BEN. We are so fucked.

> *(Blackout.)*

Scene Three (a)

(**ELIZA** *at the water color. She looks around,
surreptitious, wondering where everyone is.*)

Scene Four

(Stu's office.)

*(**WEBER** and **STU** having a drink.)*

STU. What is this stuff?

(He looks at the bottle on the desk.)

WEBER. Macallan. Like primo Macallan. Thirty years old.

STU. Holy shit. Is that smooth.

WEBER. Listen, Stu. I just wanted to touch base and let you know, this Roxbury project, we are really close to having something to show you.

STU. Great.

WEBER. I mean I am stunned that it is taking this long.

STU. Don't worry about it.

WEBER. Yeah, thanks but Stu, you gotta know that I do worry about it. I know you went out on a limb, with David, to get me positioned on this thing, and I told you I was up for it, and Ben and I, we have been at it night and day, burning the candle at both ends –

STU. I know that.

WEBER. – And honestly we are closing in on some sensational ideas, that I think are really going to knock your socks off. The client is going to be thrilled.

STU. So you think in the next couple days?

WEBER. On the outside. It's not going to take that long; we could probably make a decent presentation tomorrow, frankly. But after making you wait, I want it to be, you know. Perfect. And Janice has been a huge, well, she just came on today, so she's catching up. But she's terrific. You know, she's got a great attitude.

STU. Oh, Janice. I just, you know, I had to cover my bases on that.

WEBER. Yeah, could you explain what that's about? Because Ben alluded to something –

STU. Jesus. It's fucking moronic. And, I got to say, the whole thing makes my point, about the problem, putting women into an environment that they are not suited to.

WEBER. So Janice –

STU. Janice is fine, she's just, whatever. It's, look. This other one. I got nothing against working with women, but you get one of these, a chip on her shoulder, it's all "Oo, you don't like me because I'm a girl" –

WEBER. Oh, god. Is that what she?

STU. Of course it is. So she pulls this – Ben fill you in –

WEBER. He alluded –

STU. I mean the fact is she's David's hire.

WEBER. Yeah. I heard they were sleeping together.

STU. I'm not going to comment on that.

WEBER. Yeah. It's just what I heard.

STU. Suffice it to say we're stuck.

WEBER. Just what I heard.

STU. But as long as she's on the rampage? I'm gonna cover my bases. If she's going to make crazy accusations, who knows what else she might decide to, this stuff that's going on everywhere now, you look at one of them sideways and they're bringing you up on charges. Every other day some woman's walking off with millions. David could end up paying, which frankly would serve him right but he's not going to see it that way.

WEBER. It's crazy. This whole thing is nuts!

STU. I'm not talking about Janice. She's a team player. She won't get in your way. But if anybody decides to go to the EEOC or whatever and complain about a hostile work environment or whatever other fucking insane complaining whiny bullshit, at least we can say, look. There isn't a pattern here. There isn't grounds.

WEBER. Absolutely. I mean the shit these women are getting away with.

STU. It's fine. But that's why Janice, I had to move her over. In case this other one.

WEBER. Got it got it got it.

STU. So that's all that's about.

WEBER. Sure.

> *(Then.)*

But Ben said, that she did something, she put my name on something –

STU. You do not need to worry about that.

WEBER. Yeah but it's a little weird, you didn't tell me about it. I mean, you don't have to go into details; Ben filled me in on what happened, which was truly fucked up. He also said you were drunk!

> *(He laughs.)*

STU. He said what?

WEBER. Some bullshit, you were too drunk to even remember what she showed you.

STU. He wasn't there, so I don't think he knows.

WEBER. No, no, he was just kidding around. But you know, I wish you had just let me know. I mean, I'm involved here in a way that Ben isn't, you know, she has some sort of thing about me, personally, that's clear, and I would feel better if you had thought you could keep me in the loop. Because it's truly only been a few months, even though it feels like, your support of me here has been tremendous and I can say truthfully that already I consider you to be like a father to me. My dad's gone, you know, so this relationship, its just really important to me.

STU. Well.

WEBER. I mean it, Stu. I totally appreciate the way you support me, and I feel especially angry toward her, that she didn't respect that, that she thought that was something that she could fuck with.

STU. You got to forget people like her. She's meaningless.

WEBER. I know; I know that. But she was out there, counterfeiting my work, and then passing it off in such a way that even you would be fooled by it –

STU. I wasn't fooled.

WEBER. No, no, I know –

STU. I mean, she tricked me. But I wasn't fooled.

(He takes another drink.)

WEBER. You know what? We should forget about it. But here's my point. My point is, like, what, can you tell me what about her work, what points made you think it was mine? Because I do, Stu, I want to know, I take pride in my work and I try to make sure that whatever I do, it's as truly original as I can make it. I think about where the work stands in context to, even if it's just some fucking mall renovation, this isn't a casual enterprise in any way. The details. The philosophy. I try to make everything as specific to my vision as it can be, and if you want to call that ego, so be it, but I feel that if my name is going on it, that means that I am accountable to every aspect of the process. So if this person is out there pretending, making a phony version of who and what I am I think I have a right to ask, or even, you know, I don't think it's wrong to say that I demand to know, like what it was she did that made you think, that that was my work.

STU. I thought it was your work because it had your name on it.

WEBER. Come on, Stu. Because honestly, I don't believe that shit about you being drunk, that the reason you didn't tell Ben what she did, was that you were too drunk to remember it.

STU. Oh, that's what Ben said.

WEBER. He was kidding! He just was being, you know...

STU. No, I don't know. What's your point?

WEBER. My point is – come on, Stu! You know my work. And I'm interested in what she did, that reminded you of my work. Like maybe what she did with those ducts.

STU. I'm not so interested in telling you what she did. I'm interested in hearing what you're doing. Ben said you were having a problem with those ducts. You ever solve that?

(The two men consider each other. There is a knock on the door.)

STU. Yeah, who is it?

ELIZA. It's me! Hi. It's me.

(She sticks her head in, sees **WEBER**.*)*

Oh. I didn't know you had someone in here with you.

STU. Yeah.

ELIZA. Hey, Weber.

*(**WEBER** does not respond. He looks into his scotch glass.)*

STU. You need something?

ELIZA. I do, actually. I need to speak with you about something. Before the end of the day.

STU. It's the end of the day now.

ELIZA. Yes. It'll only take a minute.

(The two men look at her.)

It would just be great if I could have a second, Stu. There are some things I need to clear up with you. And I really would love to have the chance to do that.

STU. Seems to me there are some questions you need to clear up for both of us.

*(This startles her. She glances at **WEBER**. **WEBER** continues to stare into his glass with a deliberate and alert inattention.)*

*(**ELIZA** takes a moment and considers her options.)*

ELIZA. Okay. Fine. I'm really sorry, Stu, about what happened yesterday, and I wanted to tell you that. And I guess, you know, people know about what I did, I was frustrated, and that's no excuse, but Weber, I apologize to you, too. So I hope we can clear the air and maybe just start over.

STU. And how do you propose we do that?

ELIZA. Well, I don't, you know, I'd love to have a chance to work. On anything. Like, I know that you moved Janice over to help out on that, uh, mall thing, and I thought, she was working on that government building in Cincinnati, and I know that she probably doesn't have time to finish that now –

STU. We got it covered.

ELIZA. Okay. Sure. Well.

(To **WEBER***.)* If you need any help on anything –

WEBER. I'll let you know.

> *(She nods.)*

STU. That it?

> *(She stands there, utterly humiliated now. She sighs.)*

ELIZA. I don't know. I guess so.

> *(She takes a glass from the shelf at the side and pours herself a glass of the wildly expensive scotch.)*

What is this?

WEBER. Thirty-year-old Macallan.

ELIZA. Wow, that must cost a fucking arm and a leg.

WEBER. Yeah, it does.

> *(She downs it.)*

ELIZA. Okay. Look. Like I said, I'm sorry, you guys. But I do, I have to know where I stand here. I've been here five months and I, it's just, because this isn't going to fly anymore. And I'm having dinner with David tonight, he's been such a supporter of mine and I am going, right now, to meet him for dinner and he is going to want to know what I'm working on and I don't want to say, to him, you know, I'm not working on anything because Stu fucking hates me and I've been shut out of even the lamest fucking shitty projects he has. I don't want to tell him that.

STU. David's in Chicago. He left this morning.

ELIZA. No, he got hung up in some meeting with the clients on that restaurant thing over by the stadium, so he ended up pushing his flight till tomorrow. And he and I missed each other this morning because of course you guys were all mad at me so no one told me he was here, so when he got stuck here for an extra night he called me, and he's heading back here because he wants to have a dinner with me so he can hear about how it's going and we can catch up. So what do you want me to tell him, Stu? What the fuck do I say?

> *(She downs another drink. She and* **STU** *look at each other. Blackout.)*

End of Act One

ACT TWO

Scene Five

(The conference room. **ELIZA** *making a presentation.* **BEN, STU, WEBER,** *and* **JANICE** *listen.)*

ELIZA. What do we mean, by "governance"? When we ask, what does it mean, to be an American citizen, what do we hope is the answer? We hope that being an American citizen means fairness. Decency. Tradition. Merit. Individuality. The ideals of this country rest upon the belief that each one of us, as an individual, is a full citizen, and that what we make of ourselves, be we black, white, rich, poor, male, female – is to be honored in accordance with our achievement. Because that is fair, and decent, and traditional, and just. America, in its most profound vision of itself, is about justice. And justice is blind. In the best sense. Justice is plain. Justice is holy.

(She flicks on a light, reveals a blueprint.)

The courthouse adjunct building 3A in Montgomery Square is a small office building which is largely used for notarizations and preliminary work of a clerical nature relating to probating wills and other functions of the Surrogate's Court, next door. Our task was to address the really horrendous walkway between the buildings, replace the facade and restructure the interior to accommodate a sizable law library, which the Surrogate's Court is hoping to relocate from the main courthouse, along with two new offices, for the law librarians, as well as a kitchen, which the building has never had before. Oh, and they'd like us to expand the women's bathroom, when it was built back in 1937 there were not as many women, apparently, working in government.

I approached the substantial issues of this renovation with an eye toward simplicity and spareness in the design. In a bow to the Georgian architecture of the City of Brotherly Love, at the time of the constitutional congress, we add simple neo-classical touches to the facade, a dormer, pillars, extremely economical, but great looking, by simply repointing the brick exterior and making these few cosmetic adjustments we bring new life and focus to its identity as a building in which justice is served. The horrible walkway we remove, and replace with laid bricks under a trellis, which can be planted with ivy, or some other suitably climbing greenery. So the exterior issues can be dealt with efficiently and elegantly and economically. The questions regarding the interior are a tad more complicated. Let's take a look.

(She starts to move the top blueprint aside.)

STU. Hang on. I think this stuff on the exterior, I have some real questions about that.

ELIZA. Okay.

STU. Like, this walkway, you just took it out? How can you take it out?

ELIZA. It's a simple demolition job. It wasn't added on till the sixties anyway, and the building materials are cheap, which is why it looks so lousy –

STU. That's not what I'm talking about. It's an enclosed space, you want to take away the enclosure? Then what?

ELIZA. Then – well, you'd put doors, which used to be there, actually –

STU. You think that's the answer?

ELIZA. Doors?

STU. Answer the question.

ELIZA. I'm not sure what the question is.

STU. Anybody else have an issue with this?

(There is a pause.)

JANICE. Well – I was a little confused by the dormer.

STU. Not the dormer, the walkway. Where's the fucking walkway?

ELIZA. The walkway is not being done away with, it's being replaced with something that has an aesthetic relationship to the whole complex.

STU. I'm not talking about aesthetics.

ELIZA. Well, that's what the purpose of the renovation was, with regard to the walkway –

STU. The "purpose" of the renovation?

ELIZA. No, I know, there are a lot of things we were asked to address –

STU. Yes there were a lot of things we were asked to address, and none of them were, take out the fucking hallway between the two buildings.

ELIZA. I didn't take it out.

STU. You just said "demolition." I think I heard the word "demolition," anybody else hear that?

WEBER. I heard it. I thought, awesome, we're blowing the place up now? Fantastic.

*(He makes an explosion sound. He and **STU** laugh.)*

Don't tell the client.

(Another explosion sound. They laugh.)

ELIZA. Maybe we should look at the choices I've put in place around the interior and discuss the renovation as a whole. As I said the exterior issues are really cosmetic and economically insignificant.

STU. Demolition of a hallway is insignificant?

ELIZA. Actually, it is, Stu, and it wasn't my decision. I put a call in to the client and he said he thought it was a good idea. As long as there's pavement and a little bit of cover, he thinks that there isn't enough traffic between the two buildings to warrant hanging onto what amounts to an exterior connecting hallway. He clarified that the reason they asked us to look at it in the first place is that it's so ugly plus nobody really uses it and it was built so poorly and it's so poorly insulated that it causes terrific drafts and it's driving the heating costs way up and this would be a way of solving that but making it still convenient for people to, you know. Get from one building to another.

(There is a pause. He looks at her.)

STU. Look. I know it doesn't feel good, when you have to take criticism.

ELIZA. No, it's fine, I just –

STU. Let me finish. I can see that you've put thought into this, but honestly, on a sort of general level – and I know this is hard to hear – I just don't get it.

ELIZA. I don't know what you mean by a general level.

STU. I mean, you're too specific. Repointing bricks, neo-classical columns – it's too – specific. It's hard to relate to. People don't want to look at a building and see one thing. They want to see everything. They don't want "aesthetics," that's not what they're looking for in a government building.

ELIZA. Well, I don't think it should be ugly.

STU. I didn't say ugly. No one said ugly. You're not hearing me.

ELIZA. No, I am hearing you. I just was hoping maybe, I think some of the solutions that I came up with for the interior, which is where the real questions are –

STU. That's the thing, you rushed past the exterior and you didn't solve it.

ELIZA. There wasn't that much, it wasn't –

STU. "Demolition" isn't that much?

*(**WEBER** makes the sound of an explosion.)*

ELIZA. It's so flimsy, it's more of a tear-down –

STU. That's not what you said.

(**WEBER** *makes another explosion sound.*)

Blowing up a building is not exactly a solution.

ELIZA. That's not –

WEBER. KABOOM!

(**WEBER** *laughs.* **JANICE** *laughs.* **ELIZA** *stands there, humiliated.*)

STU. Like I said, I know it's hard to hear criticism. But if we can't get this right here, it's not going to be right for the client. And you taking it to the client, before we had a chance to vet it, was a significant breach of protocol. Significant.

ELIZA. I didn't! I called, for clarification –

STU. And talked to who?

ELIZA. I talked to – it was the person Janice had been talking to, I asked her –

STU. (*To* **JANICE**, *cool.*) You told her to go around me and talk to the client?

JANICE. No, no, of course not, I didn't – she asked me for a phone number to the urban planning office.

ELIZA. I asked who you were talking to over there and you said –

JANICE. I did not say it was all right to run ideas by that guy. He's just a clerk. I certainly never said you should call him and get clearances for whatever, demolition plans or whatever you were doing.

ELIZA. I wasn't doing anything! I wanted to touch base –

STU. Okay but why would you think that talking to some clerk over at the urban planning office would give you clearance for completely radical and unnecessary demolition? When all you were asked for was a simple plan for renovating a three-floor office building.

ELIZA. (*A beat.*) Maybe if you called over there. You could clarify it for yourself.

STU. I'm not going to call over there and talk to some clerk.

(A beat.)

BEN. Look – are we – if there is a question about whether or not that thing comes down, maybe we could clarify that and look at the rest of the design maybe tomorrow? Because I got some work to do, on those ducts. Or as long as we're all here, if anyone has any thoughts about those ducts, I'd love to hear them.

STU. We're not done with this yet.

WEBER. Yeah, I have a lot of questions about the dormer and the columns.

JANICE. I do too. I just think it's so formal and imposing.

ELIZA. It's a law building.

WEBER. They don't seem necessary to me.

ELIZA. Well, no, they're decorative –

WEBER. But it's a government building. Which is already imposing. I think especially if you repoint the bricks, it's adding a lot of texture which is kind of totalitarian Russian in feeling.

ELIZA. *(Quietly appalled and chastened.)* It's neo-classical.

STU. Look this is the discussion. This is how we work here. We're a group. You go outside the group, you try and talk to the client yourself, you act like you make all the decisions, that's not the way we do things. People are telling you things you need to listen, and incorporate the thoughts of the group. These are all smart people, you can learn things from them. If you're not interested in learning, if you're only interested in your own ego, that's going to be a problem.

(A beat.)

ELIZA. Of course I'm interested in learning.

STU. Great. Let's get to work! Janice, what are your thoughts about the dormer.

JANICE. It seems unnecessary and like I said, the formality bothers me. For a legal building you want to put people at ease. I was working on a different approach, which I understand why you threw out everything I did on this, when you needed to step in and take it over, I don't have a problem with that, but I did a lot of thinking about it and there are just a few obvious steps. Like, a coat of paint.

    (Blackout.)

Scene Six

(Janice's office. Next day. **ELIZA** *is there alone.*
JANICE *enters, sees her.)*

JANICE. Oh! Hi!

ELIZA. *(Cool.)* Hi.

JANICE. Can I help you?

ELIZA. Can you "help" me?

JANICE. I'm sorry, I'm just really busy right now. We're really under the gun on this mall thing.

ELIZA. Not going so well?

JANICE. No! It's going great. Really great. We're about to show it to Stu. David is coming back in town and he wants to be able to present.

ELIZA. You ever solve the duct thing?

JANICE. Absolutely.

ELIZA. Oh yeah what'd you do?

JANICE. It's complicated.

ELIZA. I didn't think so. Not once you figure it out. It's like those optical illusions, you get so used to seeing the thing one way, you never notice that it's this whole other thing. The lady or the cup. It's all point of view.

JANICE. Well, we have a terrific solution.

ELIZA. Does Ben think that?

JANICE. You spoke with Ben?

ELIZA. No. I just wondered if he agrees with you. That you have a terrific solution.

JANICE. Absolutely.

ELIZA. That means no.

JANICE. Look.

ELIZA. So you and *Ronald* like whatever lame-ass idea you came up with last night at three in the morning, but Ben doesn't and he knows that when you guys show it to David you guys are going to get hammered. *Hammered.*

JANICE. I'm not the one who's getting hammered around here. Now, if you don't mind.

ELIZA. If I don't mind what?

JANICE. Forget it. I have to go.

ELIZA. I need to talk to you.

JANICE. I'm sorry, I just don't have time.

ELIZA. I need to talk to you about what went down yesterday, in that presentation.

JANICE. Another time would be better.

ELIZA. Because I really, really did not appreciate the way you undermined me.

JANICE. I did not undermine anything!

ELIZA. I came to you. I came to you and asked you for the background on that fucking law building –

JANICE. And I gave you everything you asked for –

ELIZA. And you told me to call that guy. That guy is not a clerk! He's the project liason! You told me to call him!

JANICE. I didn't tell you to call him.

ELIZA. You did! You most certainly did, you said –

JANICE. Look, I know it doesn't feel good when your work isn't received well.

ELIZA. No it doesn't it feels shitty especially when the one person in the office who maybe could support you shoots you in the fucking back.

(A beat.)

JANICE. I tried to help you. I did. You came in here, and you expected what did you expect? You came in like you were better than everyone

ELIZA. That's why they hired me! They told me up front that I was going to have to be eight times as good as the fucking boneheads they normally hire; well, when you hire a woman eight times as good that's what you end up with! A woman who's eight times as good as everyone else!

JANICE. You clearly weren't good enough to take over my project.

ELIZA. I didn't –

JANICE. You went to Stu and asked for it! Everyone in the building knows it!

ELIZA. How is it your project? You said yourself you hadn't done anything on it!

JANICE. There's no deadline on that thing and we're getting paid shit for it anyway –

ELIZA. That is my point I went after it because I thought, JESUS I thought it might be insignificant enough that –

JANICE. But EVERYONE has projects like that laying around their offices.

ELIZA. Everyone except for me!

JANICE. And you didn't go after them, did you? You didn't go after Weber, or Ben. You went after me. Because I'm the other girl. You thought you'd get away with it because you were only poaching from a *girl*. And now I'm supposed to feel bad, I didn't stand up for you in that meeting because you're the other *girl* and we should be sticking together? Screw you. They expect us to stick together and you expect me to be your sidekick. I love that. I've been here six years, you come in and in five months you've got everyone completely pissed off and I'm supposed to stand up for you because we both have breasts and a vagina. Look why don't we just go shopping together? That'll solve everything.

ELIZA. That's not –

JANICE. I told you to keep your mouth shut! I told you to give him time, I told you how to handle him –

ELIZA. Handle him, why do I have to handle all these cocksuckers! I came here to work! I was hired to work!

JANICE. Yeah, well no one wants to work with you, so that's a problem.

ELIZA. That isn't my fault.

JANICE. You're a malcontent.

ELIZA. Of course I'm a malcontent they shoved me in a corner and ignored me for FIVE FUCKING MONTHS! ONLY A FUCKING IDIOT WOULD BE CONTENTED WITH THAT.

JANICE. Look, I got a meeting to go to. Oh! And you don't.

ELIZA. They think you're an idiot, Janice! They put you on that mall thing because they know I solved it and Stu is too fucked up to admit it, because he doesn't like it that I'm smarter than he is and I'm a WOMAN so they put you on it instead of me to prove that they don't have a problem with women! Get a clue! You're their beard! They love women who are incompetent and mediocre because it makes it easier to dismiss them! When someone really good shows up they shove her in a corner and say she's got an attitude problem.

JANICE. You do have an attitude problem.

ELIZA. I do now, there's no question about that, my attitude fucking sucks now.

JANICE. And frankly, I don't think I am the one they're dismissing. Looks to me like you are.

(There is a knock on the door.)

(Lovely.) Come in!

*(**BEN** sticks his head in.)*

BEN. Hey.

JANICE. Hi, you heading over?

BEN. No, I just got a call from Stu's office. He's stuck on a call, going to be another twenty minutes. So we still got twenty minutes to try to figure out that duct thing. Anybody got any ideas.

*(He looks at **ELIZA**. She smiles at him.)*

JANICE. I like what we came up with! I think it's a terrific approach.

BEN. Oh yeah. I just meant, it's always worth, you know.

(Then.)

See you over there.

(He goes, shutting the door behind him.)

JANICE. I really need you to go.

ELIZA. You have twenty minutes.

JANICE. And I need them to prepare.

ELIZA. Yeah you do because you don't have it.

JANICE. Look –

ELIZA. Do you want it?

JANICE. We don't need it.

ELIZA. Oh yes you do! Ben just walked in here and admitted it!

JANICE. Ben is very conservative in his approach to things.

ELIZA. Ben is the only person around here who knows what he's doing.

JANICE. Aside from you.

ELIZA. Yes, aside from me. Do you want it?

JANICE. You're ridiculous.

ELIZA. Maybe not so much. Come on, do you want it?

(A beat.)

Janice. Why are you even considering this?

JANICE. I'm not!

ELIZA. Yes you are; you're thinking about it. That means two things. One, you know that what you guys came up with sucks. Two, you know that what I came up with works.

JANICE. How would I know or care what you came up with?

ELIZA. 'Cause you heard about it. Stu saw it.

JANICE. If Stu's seen it why doesn't he just take credit for it?

ELIZA. He can't remember it! What's left of his brain is pickled in scotch. And that's not even the real problem, the real problem is, it came from me.

Even if he could remember it, he'd be stealing from me, and he won't give me the satisfaction. But if you saved his ass on this, he might be pretty happy about that.

JANICE. I thought he had a "big problem" with women.

ELIZA. He doesn't have a problem with you because you're a Nazi collaborator.

JANICE. And you wonder why people don't like you.

ELIZA. Do you want it?

JANICE. You're offering to give it to me.

ELIZA. Yes I am.

JANICE. Why?

ELIZA. *(A beat.)* Because I would like to see something I designed, built. I don't care if my name is on it. I don't care if I get credit for it. I don't care. That fucking asshole, accusing me of having too much ego, I don't care! I want to work! I want to see the work done. Take it. Put your name on it. Take credit for it. Build it. It's the solution.

> *(She reaches into the corner behind her and pulls out a rolled-up blueprint. She holds it out.)*

JANICE. I don't...

ELIZA. You don't believe me, you don't think you know enough, go show it to Ben. He'll tell you, it's good. It's elegant.

JANICE. You think I don't know enough?

ELIZA. No. No! I just meant, Ben will, Ben –

JANICE. Ben doesn't know everything.

ELIZA. No, I know.

JANICE. Besides which, I think what we've got works.

ELIZA. Do you?

JANICE. Yes. I do! Ronald really likes it.

ELIZA. *(A gentle reminder.)* Janice – he's a colossal moron.

JANICE. We both like what we came up with!

ELIZA. *(A beat.)* Could at least, just to humor me, could you – look at it?

> *(She stands there, humble, with the blueprint.)*

JANICE. The meeting starts –

ELIZA. You have time to look at it.

> (**JANICE** *looks at her. After a moment,* **ELIZA** *unrolls the blueprint and pins it to Janice's drawing board. She steps aside.* **JANICE** *goes to it and looks. She stops. There is a long pause as she studies it.*)

Scene Seven

*(Stu's office. **JANICE** is at the doorway, holding the design and a cup of coffee. **STU** is at his desk.)*

JANICE. Hi.

STU. Janice! Didn't anybody call you? We bumped.

JANICE. Ben mentioned you were stuck on a call but then I saw that you were off and I thought I'd grab you for five minutes. That's okay I hope.

STU. Well.

JANICE. Five minutes.

STU. Yeah, I got five minutes.

(She puts the coffee on his desk.)

JANICE. Half and half no sugar right?

STU. Not supposed to be doing the half and half anymore. My wife, you should hear her.

JANICE. Oh –

(She is unsure if she should take the coffee back. He waves her off.)

STU. No no no, please. A little bit of half and half, how bad can it be? I mean, it's ridiculous. Although I hope you're not going to turn this into some big, because I didn't ask you to bring me coffee.

JANICE. *(Laughing.)* No no no, that's, I brought you coffee of my own free will. You're in the clear.

STU. Good.

JANICE. You know I don't have those kinds of issues. This is my workplace and my position is we have enough to do without a lot of crazy politics.

STU. You're unique in that respect these days. So thank you for saying that.

JANICE. I'm sorry that it has to be said! It seems obvious.

STU. Well.

*(**STU** checks his watch.)*

JANICE. I know we only have a minute. But I did want to see if there was a time that maybe you and I could talk about my standing. Here at the firm.

STU. Your standing is great.

JANICE. Good, thanks, good. But you know we haven't, I haven't had a review in a couple years.

STU. Has it been that long?

JANICE. It has, actually it has. And I haven't had a raise for more than two years.

STU. Oh here we go.

JANICE. *(Laughing.)* Well, yes, that's –

STU. I'm just going to be frank. This is not a great time for you to bring this up. There are a lot of problems on my plate right now. This Eliza Newsom, she's not doing you any favors.

JANICE. Me? I don't have anything to do with her.

STU. You know what I mean.

JANICE. She's not doing anyone any favors.

STU. That's for damn sure.

JANICE. And that's not to say anything bad about her. It just seems clear that it's not a great fit. For you or her.

STU. I got no problem with her.

JANICE. I just mean she's not really a team player. And this is not the right environment for that sort of thing. I like her so much. I'm just aware that sometimes situations just don't work out. Through nobody's fault. And I really do see how hard everybody has been working to make this successful. I'm so impressed with how you've been handling it. I thought it was so gracious of you, after what she did with that other situation around the Roxbury mall project which was absolutely inappropriate, it was really shocking to me when I heard about the way she...

STU. Did she talk to you about that?

JANICE. No. No. No. I heard about it from Weber, who is I think rightly really upset but being a total team player, and everyone is so impressed with how you handled that, that in the face of something so inappropriate you took her under your wing and put her on the law office that I had been working on, that was really great mentoring on your part. You've gone so above and beyond.

STU. Has she been complaining about me?

JANICE. Well – I think everybody knows she's not happy. But she's not a happy person, in general.

STU. I heard you kind of got into it with her today.

JANICE. Oh.

STU. It's not a big office. When people raise their voices, you hear it.

JANICE. Well I really did not appreciate how she's been handling any of this. And I let her know it. I'm on your side, Stu.

STU. Thanks.

JANICE. That's why I wanted to touch base. I'm doing my best, and I will continue to try and make this work with her, because that is my job. And I will tell anyone who asks how you stood up to a really complicated personnel issue and how much we appreciated your leadership.

STU. And you want a raise.

JANICE. Well – I would like a review, for sure.

STU. It's just weird that you're being kind of aggressive here.

JANICE. Aggressive – no –

STU. I mean we both know I've got my hands full with this trouble that frankly the one other woman who works for me, has created.

JANICE. I don't –

STU. Just honestly your timing could be better. I mean I appreciate your coming in here and expressing your support, I really do. But this other issue, let's pick a different time.

JANICE. Absolutely.

STU. Thanks.

JANICE. Although you know – there are a lot of other women who work for you. All of the assistants are women.

>*(She smiles at him, making a joke out of it. He isn't amused.)*

STU. I wasn't talking about them.

JANICE. No. I know.

STU. Look, we got to get to the conference room so I can find out what you guys have come up with, on that mall thing.

JANICE. Just. Before you do.

STU. Janice, make an appointment with Molly, we'll review your compensation but I'm just going to say it again this isn't a great time to bring this up.

JANICE. *(Pushing through.)* I did some work. On those ducts. I think you should take a look at it.

STU. Bring it to the meeting.

JANICE. I didn't want to bring it to the meeting. I wanted to bring it to you. Because I think that you will know what to do with it.

STU. Jesus you women are pushy. Let me see it, let me see it.

>*(She holds it out. He looks at her. Cautious, she presents it. He looks at it.)*
>
>*(Blackout.)*

Scene Eight

(The water cooler. **WEBER** *and* **ELIZA**.*)*

WEBER. Hey! Eliza Newsom. Getting some water.

ELIZA. Yeah. I'm getting water.

WEBER. How are you feeling about your presentation yesterday?

ELIZA. How am I feeling?

WEBER. Yeah, you feeling good about it? I thought you got some terrific feedback.

ELIZA. I'm still working it through.

WEBER. It doesn't sound like there's any rush on it. You can take your time.

ELIZA. Thanks. I guess you're presenting any minute now. That's what Janice told me.

WEBER. That's the plan.

ELIZA. Ben says you still haven't licked that duct thing.

WEBER. No. No! No, we have some really great thoughts about it.

ELIZA. Thoughts?

WEBER. We have a few little holes to plug, but –

ELIZA. "Holes"?

WEBER. There are always holes. You know that.

ELIZA. Totally. It's just a slightly nerve-racking metaphor when you're talking about ducts. It's so easy for a little hole to turn into a big hole.

WEBER. I'm not really worried about that.

ELIZA. No?

WEBER. We have so many great things to talk about, so many great directions, thoughts, areas, the design aspect is really huge on this. The duct thing, that's really just the mingy stuff. You get a good mechanical engineer or even a general contractor, he'll figure that out.

ELIZA. Mingy? The ducts are "mingy"?

WEBER. Oh – sorry. I know you have a special affection for those ducts.

ELIZA. No no.

WEBER. No come on. Everyone knows. You have a little hard-on for those ducts.

ELIZA. I just never thought of architecture that way. I don't – I don't think any part is mingy. I like all of it. Every line has a meaning.

WEBER. Which is great. Just, for me, I don't want to get all tangled up in details that are like – I like what Stu said yesterday. The specifics could really drown you. The vision is where the excitement is. I think we're going to really blow David away.

And then I have to be honest, I have my eye on what he's doing. I stopped by his office this morning. Just to say hello, touch base, and wow! He has some great stuff in the works.

ELIZA. David?

WEBER. Am I stepping in your territory?

ELIZA. No! No. No.

WEBER. From what I can see, I think you're safe in that area.

ELIZA. You're going to miss your meeting.

WEBER. Not a chance. See you on the other side Newsom.

ELIZA. Good luck.

> (*He goes. She feels sick.*)

> (*Stu's office.* **BEN** *in the doorway, looking around.* **STU** *enters.*)

STU. There you are! I was just going to call you.

BEN. Yeah, what happened?

STU. What didn't happen. This day, I'm telling you.

> (*He gets out scotch bottle and pours them both a drink.*)

BEN. 'Cause when you didn't show up for the presentation, I was like what the fuck –

STU. Look there wasn't time. David's upstairs, having a hernia about who knows what.

BEN. Not about this mall thing?

STU. Well, yes, about this mall thing, this mall thing is a huge fucking – that thing is a six million dollar project, what are you talking about "this fucking mall thing"? He's mystified, what the fuck is taking so long, the client wants his fucking retainer back.

BEN. Oh Jesus.

STU. That's right, you fucked me, you fucker.

BEN. Stu, I have been trying to tell you –

STU. Don't even start; I know you got nothing.

BEN. That's not true –

STU. It is true! I check in with Weber every day and he's –

BEN. Weber? You check in with Weber?

STU. That a problem?

BEN. Is it a "problem" that you asked Weber to spy on me?

STU. Oh, Jesus.

BEN. Well, what are you saying? He's bringing some story to you every day, behind my back –

STU. He's keeping me in the loop, how you're doing with that fucking mall thing.

BEN. What, am I supposed to like this?

STU. I don't care if you like it or not. I would prefer if you didn't act like a big fucking baby about it.

BEN. Stu –

STU. Cool your jets. Nobody's after your balls. Everything is just fucked and tense because of this this this –

BEN. I actually don't think –

STU. You don't think what? You don't think she's a problem?

BEN. No, she's clearly a problem but I'd just really like to discuss this mall situation, Stu.

STU. That mall situation is handled.

BEN. It's not handled. We need to discuss it.

STU. Oh you want to discuss it.

BEN. Yes. Because no matter what we do, no matter how many different ways we look at it, it all comes back to the ducts.

STU. I don't want to hear about those fucking ducts.

BEN. You got to hear about them, Stu, and you have to hear about them from me, because they are at the center of everything. Those ducts are like a disease. They are a goiter. They are a cancerous fucking tumor on the southeast entrance of that fucking mall, and they are threatening to bring the whole place down, and now they're growing, the trouble they have caused us does not cease, it spreads, and now it's spreading here, through our offices, into our hearts, we're in trouble here, all of us, we're turning on each other and suspicious of each other and why? Because of those ducts. And the thing is – the thing is, Stu – we can stop it. We know what to do about it.

STU. Did you hear about the catfight those two had going in Janice's office?

BEN. Stu, we own the answer.

STU. She-devil alert!

BEN. Even if she left now, even if she LEFT she couldn't take it with her. It's not her intellectual property. The company owns everything in the building. We can just go into her office and take it.

STU. I don't need to take anything from her.

BEN. Stu!

STU. SHE HAS NOTHING. You're right about that, boy. She doesn't have the answer, and she doesn't own the answer and she's not so fucking smart, either. Not by a long shot.

> *(He tosses a rolled-up blueprint on the table before them.)*

BEN. What's this.

STU. What's this. "What's this"? Look at it, you want to know what it is.

> *(**BEN** looks at him, unrolls the blueprint. He looks at **STU**.)*

BEN. Where did you get this?

STU. I'll tell you where I got it. From my head.

BEN. From your –

STU. FROM. MY. HEAD. I got sick of waiting for you and your fucking minions to come up with some sort of lame-ass solution to this situation. I gave you your fucking shot, and you left me with my balls hanging in the wind, so I went back and looked at the specs, and I did it myself. All right? I did it myself.

> (**BEN** *looks at the drawing. A long moment.*
> **BEN** *looks up.*)

BEN. You did this?

STU. That so hard to believe?

BEN. No! NO. No.

STU. Yeah. So I solved it. And I took it to David, and I told him what a fucking pain in the ass his little protégé has been around here, and how much trouble she's caused, and I know he's sleeping with her, everyone knows it.

BEN. You said that?

STU. Of course I didn't say it but I implied it. I implied it! I said we all did our best. We wanted her to work out. But she brings nothing. We don't need her and she is nothing.

BEN. And you showed him this.

STU. Why shouldn't I? I've put up with him and his fucking BULLSHIT for long enough, the guy's a fucking, he's never here! And then he breezes in and out like, like who the fuck gave him that fucking deal? He acts like the Queen of fucking Sheba, prancing around like some sort of Christ you know, this whole company is all his wife's money. And who runs this place? Day in and day out, and we're, what, he can't even be bothered to, this is beneath him, but I'm here. Every day. Making it work. The mall renovations. And the chain restaurants. And the re-imagined subdivisions. Everything that's beneath his notice. And he's going to shove that bitch down my throat? Why should I put up with that shit? Why should I?

(He looks at **BEN***, furious.)*

BEN. No reason at all.

STU. That's right.

BEN. So David probably didn't have a chance to look at this, yet.

STU. What's your point, Ben?

BEN. Just, I'm curious what he said. He must've been pretty happy. To see this.

STU. He was.

BEN. But he didn't have a chance, in the moment, to look at it.

STU. I just said. We ran it through the copying machine and got it straight to him. He's looking at it now.

(The phone rings. The two men look at it. **BEN** *stands.)*

BEN. I guess you're going to need to get that.

*(***BEN*** goes to the door.)*

STU. Yeah, hi.

(Then.)

Sure, put him through.

*(***BEN*** watches from the door. Blackout.)*

Scene Nine

(Eliza's office.)

(She is putting things in a box. **BEN** *stands in her doorway. He carries a rolled-up blueprint.)*

BEN. Hey.

ELIZA. *(Looking up.)* Oh. Hi.

BEN. What're you doing?

ELIZA. What does it look like.

(She continues packing.)

BEN. You going somewhere.

ELIZA. Am I going somewhere. Yes, I seem to be quitting, so yes.

(She continues packing. **BEN** *sits across from her.)*

BEN. You never went back for this after your presentation yesterday. I was sitting in there and I had a chance to really look at it. It's good.

ELIZA. *(Barely acknowledging this.)* Thanks.

*(***BEN** *unrolls it. She looks to the ceiling, annoyed. He is focused on the drawing.)*

BEN. I'm sorry we never got to talk about what you came up with on the interiors. That's where the real skill shines, it's so ingenious what you did, breaking the floor through so the library has this corner atrium.

(He glances up at her, rolls it back up.)

The only real problem with that presentation was the beginning. You should've skipped the little speech and gotten right to it. All that crap about justice and individuality. The little dig you dropped in about how everybody's equal under the law, even women. It pissed him off.

ELIZA. Yet another thing that's my fault. That little comment about justice and equality. Really crossed the line.

BEN. This thing you do, the crosshatching in the lower left-hand corner, four and three, when'd you start doing that, in college?

ELIZA. Why?

BEN. It's like your tell, huh? Your mark. So even if your name's not on it, what?

ELIZA. Why don't you tell me "what," Ben.

BEN. It's an old drafting trick. You studied with someone pretty traditional and then you never broke the habit because you liked it. All this piecemeal work we do now, or the teams! Everybody collaborating on shit that is totally corporatized junk, you still want your mark somewhere. You were the one who had the idea for that pretty little atrium. Your secret mark in the corner. Someone like me just might notice.

ELIZA. Like I said...

BEN. The other thing I noticed, Stu's got a design sitting on his desk, with his name on it. He claims he licked that problem with the ducts. He's got a solution in there came right out of his head.

ELIZA. Good for him.

BEN. With your mark on it.

ELIZA. Well, that is weird.

BEN. Want to know what's even weirder? The design is shit. It doesn't solve a fucking thing. It looks pretty but all the cooling vents are going to end up blasting carbon dioxide all over the food court and freon all over the entryway.

ELIZA. Really? Wow. Did you tell Stu?

BEN. Too late. He already took it to David. Got so excited by what he pulled off, he wanted credit for it right away.

ELIZA. And what did David say?

BEN. I don't know what David said. I imagine he's going to tell Stu he doesn't know what the fuck he's doing.

ELIZA. Oh well.

BEN. Doubt he'll get fired. But he'll definitely be embarrassed.

ELIZA. Oh well.

   (**BEN** *watches her pack.*)

BEN. So that's it? That's what you did with the ducts? That lame-ass bullshit? I been killing myself trying to figure it out, and the solution is there's no solution?

ELIZA. There's a solution. Just not the one Stu has on his desk.

   (*She reaches into the middle of the rolls behind her, finds one, hands it to him. He looks at her, looks at it, unrolls it. He studies it. She watches him study it, gets two glasses and a bottle out of her desk, pours them both drinks while he considers the design. He looks up at her.*)

BEN. This is...impressive.

ELIZA. Thank you.

BEN. This isn't what Stu has.

ELIZA. No he has my third draft, it's largely stupid. I didn't crack it until draft number seven but I convinced Janice that one was what you guys were all looking for and then *she* took it to Stu.

BEN. Janice did.

ELIZA. Yes she did. She thought it might score her some points to bring Stu the holy grail.

BEN. And you told her not to let me see it.

ELIZA. Well, Ben, quite frankly, you're the only one around here who might have noticed that it's shit.

BEN. And you didn't want that. You wanted Janice to take the fall.

ELIZA. Janice is fine.

BEN. David is up there reaming out Stu, somebody's going to have to pay for that.

ELIZA. Poor thing.

BEN. She never hurt anybody.

ELIZA. She hurt me. In that meeting yesterday, she could have stood up for me but she didn't; she stabbed me in the back and left me hung out to dry. Oh, but that's okay, isn't it? As long as she doesn't give you guys trouble, "she's never hurt anybody."

BEN. That why you did it? To take revenge on Janice?

ELIZA. What is it I did again? No. Let me tell you what I did. I came to work. And even when I was being shut out, I worked hard. I SHOWED him that design. I showed it to him and he couldn't even remember it. He was too busy condescending and dismissing and shoving me into a fucking broom closet –

BEN. Grow up. Stu is an old drunk and this job is all he's got and you worked his nerves.

ELIZA. I "worked his nerves"?

BEN. Tell me if I got this wrong. You went into his office and told him you were meeting with David, who everyone assumes you are sleeping with –

ELIZA. I am not sleeping with David –

BEN. Who gives a shit if you are or not, it's what they think and you are letting them think that –

ELIZA. I'm not LETTING them think anything –

BEN. And then you go in there and you threaten him –

ELIZA. I was at the end of my rope!

BEN. Maybe you were. This shit, however, was a little more deliberate.

(He taps the drawing on the desk.)

ELIZA. Yeah, well maybe someone around here should have given me something to do once in a while. I clearly have too much time on my hands.

BEN. Look. I was on your side.

ELIZA. You weren't on my side. You could have been. You could have thrown me a bone once in a while. But you didn't want to rock the boat. Weber came in, Stu was all infatuated with that – why do they fall for those shitheads? God. Everywhere I go, these fucking golden boys with their architalk! What is it about a pretty boy with no brain that makes all these shitheads with power start singing love songs? Do they see themselves in these talent-free idiots? Oh who cares. But that's what happened. Weber came in, you felt a little threatened, so you stuck with the party line, keep the girls in their place. Don't go telling yourself you're the nice guy, Ben. You could have done something and you didn't. That doesn't make you nice. That makes you a coward.

BEN. And why was I supposed to stick my neck out for you? Because of your charm?

ELIZA. Because it was the right thing to do! I came here, you stuck me in a closet, and expected me to just take it. You tried to erase me. Well you can erase me all you want, but you cannot erase *that*. That is real. My talent is as real as as as a *tree*.

(*A beat.*)

BEN. Come on. Let's get out of here. Let's go get something to eat.

ELIZA. You want me to have dinner with you?

BEN. I do, yeah.

ELIZA. Wait a minute. Are you asking me for a fucking date? That's *just* what this workplace needs.

BEN. Come on. Let's get out of here before this gets any worse. This has been nobody's smartest or most shining hour. I'm done for today with the fall of man. Let's get out of here.

(*A beat.*)

ELIZA. Christ. I don't know, Ben. What would we even talk about?

BEN. Ducts. Man, I'd really like to talk about –

(**STU** *enters, furious. He throws a rolled-up design onto Eliza's desk. Glares at her.*)

STU. In my office. Now.

      (He goes. **ELIZA** *looks back at* **BEN**, *shrugs.)*

      (She goes. After a moment, **BEN** *sits. Lights shift.)*

Scene Ten

(Eliza's office. Ten minutes later. **BEN** *is still sitting there.* **WEBER** *sticks his head in, looks around.)*

WEBER. Hey! What are you doing back here?

BEN. Nothing.

WEBER. Where is everybody?

BEN. I don't know.

WEBER. Geez, this is a little office.

BEN. It is.

WEBER. This place is a broom closet. My office has a wet bar.

BEN. That's a lateral file.

WEBER. Call it whatever you want. She is not going to last. This one.

> *(***STU*** *and* ***ELIZA*** *enter.)*

Stu I was just looking for you. I had some ideas about that duct thing that I think are really super promising.

> *(***ELIZA*** *goes to her desk, rolls up the good design, and hands it to* ***STU.****)*

STU. This is the right one?

Because as I think I told you, David is not amused by any of this.

ELIZA. That's the design.

STU. And you're done with all this, this –

ELIZA. I'm done.

STU. Whatever it is. You're done?

ELIZA. I'm done.

> *(She reaches into her desk and pulls out a couple of glasses and a bottle. She pours* **STU** *a drink, pours herself one, and offers his to him.)*
>
> *(He looks at her, suspicious.)*

It's not cyanide, Stu. I promise.

(They both drink. **WEBER** *sticks his head back in the doorway.)*

WEBER. So, you two are just burying the hatchet?

STU. Yeah. I'm putting her on the mall renovation. She's going to work it with Ben.

WEBER. Oh. Whoa, really?

STU. You got a problem?

WEBER. Well, I just – yeah, I actually do. I mean we were getting close to some pretty interesting things, I thought.

STU. The client's not interested in close.

WEBER. Well, but –

STU. David's not interested in close either. She and Ben have a pretty good handle on it. So I'm going to let them run with it. David is going to want to hear from you both tomorrow.

ELIZA. Got it.

STU. Get to work.

WEBER. I mean, can we talk about this? Because I put a lot of myself into that project. I mean, my work is just all over that thing. No offense, Eliza. I mean I've been on it for months.

STU. And now she's on it. Her and Ben. BEN.

*(***BEN*** *holds his hand out, and* ***STU*** *hands him the design.* ***STU*** *leaves;* ***WEBER*** *follows.)*

WEBER. So let me know what you need, guys. I'm here for you. Stu! Stu!

(He goes. ***BEN*** *and* ***ELIZA*** *are left alone.)*

BEN. I guess that went all right.

ELIZA. Very professional.

BEN. As always.

(He heads for the door.)

This place is a broom closet. We'll work in my office. I'll send out for sandwiches.

*(***JANICE*** *appears in the doorway.)*

JANICE. We're working late?

BEN. Oh. Janice.

JANICE. So did Stu show the design to David?

ELIZA. Nobody talked to you?

JANICE. Did he like it?

BEN. I'll let Eliza fill you in.

> *(He goes.* **JANICE** *waits, looks at* **ELIZA**. *Shuts the door. She is friendly, conspiratorial, excited.)*

JANICE. So I heard Weber talking to Stu in the hall. I gather he is off the mall project and not happy about it, either.

ELIZA. No, he didn't seem to be.

JANICE. And you're on it! That's a surprise. Because trust me I did not mention where that design came from.

ELIZA. No, I know you didn't.

JANICE. So what happened?

ELIZA. Nobody called you?

JANICE. No! What happened?

ELIZA. It's complicated. Wow, I wish Stu had called you.

JANICE. You're making me nervous.

ELIZA. Okay it's kind of hard to explain.

> *(A beat.)*

Stu – that design I gave you – it's not really the one everyone was looking for.

> *(A beat.)*

JANICE. What do you mean?

ELIZA. I gave you the wrong one. That one was an earlier draft, it had a lot of mistakes in it. And Stu showed it to David, who got mad. And then we just sorted it out. And now they have the right one.

JANICE. You gave me an earlier draft. With mistakes in it.

ELIZA. Yeah.

JANICE. And you told me to tell Stu that I had designed it. The one with all the mistakes.

ELIZA. I was confused.

JANICE. Confused? So you gave me the design with all the mistakes in it by accident?

ELIZA. Not – strictly, by accident –

JANICE. I see. You let me take the wrong design and embarrass him so that then I could take the blame for that.

ELIZA. That's not what I –

JANICE. Sure it is. Sure it is! And you got what you wanted. Well, good for you. You got that stupid mall. Congratulations. Although I have to tell you, it's not all that. Lest we forget – it's a MALL. And there are still a million issues with that thing. We're going to be here all night.

    (She stands, heads for the door.)

ELIZA. Janice, that's not –

JANICE. It's not what, true? Everything I just said isn't true? You threw me under the bus, that's not true?

ELIZA. You should go home.

JANICE. I CAN'T go home. I just heard Ben say it. We have to pull an all-nighter on that stupid...

    *(She stops. Looks at **ELIZA**, shakes her head.)*

ELIZA. You really should just go home.

JANICE. I'm not on it, am I.

ELIZA. He didn't say.

JANICE. Did you ask him?

    (Silence.)

Did you tell him, that you were the one who gave me the design with the mistakes in it, did you tell him that? And did you say, it's not Janice's fault, I told her to bring you the shitty early draft of what to do with those fucking ducts –

ELIZA. There wasn't actually a moment that was appropriate –

JANICE. Why am I not surprised.

ELIZA. I'm sorry.

JANICE. Don't tell me you're sorry. You're not sorry.

ELIZA. I am sorry.

JANICE. This is fucked.

ELIZA. Janice.

JANICE. This is FUCKED. I'm going to lose my job. I am, I'm going to lose my job.

ELIZA. He did not say that.

JANICE. You can be all smug about it.

ELIZA. I'm hardly smug.

JANICE. You hated me from the moment you laid eyes on me! Why? Because I play ball. Well, somebody had to play ball with those fuckers. It was the only way to stay in the room. But we did stay there and we held the fucking door open so that you could waltz in and be equal. And now you want to slam it in my face? You don't know what that means? When they don't tell you things? When they just leave you out of meetings? When you're always begging for information? You're going to tell me you don't know what that means?

ELIZA. I just wanted to work!

JANICE. If you say that one more time I am going to punch you in the face.

    (A silence. The two women sit there together.)

Why is it still like this?

ELIZA. I don't know.

JANICE. Me neither.

    (They sit there, thinking about that.)
    (Blackout.)

End of Play

CPSIA information can be obtained
at www.ICGtesting.com
Printed in the USA
LVHW082135100822
725695LV00027B/943